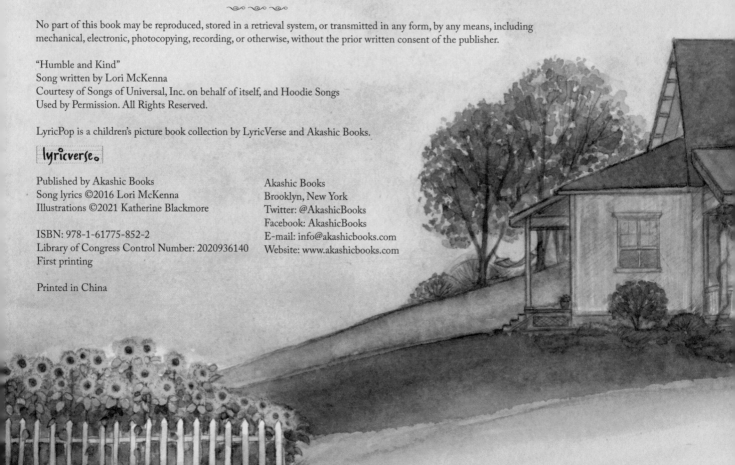

Becky Fluke

Lori McKenna is a singer-songwriter who has emerged as one of the most respected, prolific artists in popular music. Her 2016 release *The Bird and the Rifle* netted three GRAMMY nominations, along with Americana Music Association nods. In 2016, she became the first woman ever to win the Country Music Association's Song of the Year two years in a row, thanks to cowriting Little Big Town's "Girl Crush" and penning the #1 hit song "Humble and Kind." Both songs also clinched back-to-back GRAMMY Awards for Best Country Song. In 2017, she became the Academy of Country Music's first female Songwriter of the Year. *The Tree*, her much-anticipated eleventh studio album, was released in 2018 on CN Records via Thirty Tigers.

KATHERINE BLACKMORE's (illustrator) professional career spans over twenty-five years of illustrating, animating, and teaching. Her work has been featured in products for American Greetings, animated films for Disney, and several children's picture books. She currently teaches kids in the Creative Core Art Program, which she founded. She lives in Orlando with her husband.

"Humble and Kind"
Song written by Lori McKenna
Courtesy of Songs of Universal, Inc. on behalf of itself, and Hoodie Songs
Used by Permission. All Rights Reserved.

LyricPop is a children's picture book collection by LyricVerse and Akashic Books.

lyricverse。

Published by Akashic Books
Song lyrics ©2016 Lori McKenna
Illustrations ©2021 Katherine Blackmore

ISBN: 978-1-61775-852-2
Library of Congress Control Number: 2020936140
First printing

Printed in China

Akashic Books
Brooklyn, New York
Twitter: @AkashicBooks
Facebook: AkashicBooks
E-mail: info@akashicbooks.com
Website: www.akashicbooks.com

humble
and
kind

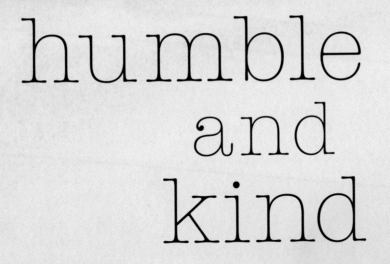

song lyrics by
Lori McKenna

illustrations by
Katherine Blackmore

You know there's a light that glows by the front door.

Don't forget, the key's under the mat.

When childhood stars shine,

always stay humble and kind.

Go to church 'cause your momma says to.

Visit grandpa every chance that you can.

It won't be wasted time.

Always stay humble and kind.

Hold the door . . .

say please, say thank you.

Don't steal, don't cheat, and don't lie.

I know you got mountains to climb,
but always stay humble and kind.

When the dreams that you're dreamin' come to you.

When the work you put in is realized.

Let yourself feel the pride,

but always stay humble and kind.

Don't expect a free ride from no one.

Don't hold a grudge or a chip

and here's why...

Bitterness keeps you from flyin'.

Always stay humble and kind.

Know the difference between sleepin' with someone,

and sleepin' with someone you love.

"I love you" ain't no pickup line,

so always stay humble and kind.

Hold the door, say please, say thank you.

Don't steal, don't cheat, and don't lie.

I know you got mountains to climb,

but always stay humble and kind.

When those dreams that you're dreamin' come to you.

When the work you put in is realized.

Let yourself feel the pride,

but always stay humble and kind.

When it's hot, eat a root beer Popsicle.

Shut off the AC and roll the windows down.

And let the summer sun shine.

Always stay humble and kind.

Don't take for granted

the love this life gives you.

When you get where you're goin'
turn right back around,
and help the next one in line.

LOOK OUT FOR THESE LyricPop TITLES

The 59th Street Bridge Song (Feelin' Groovy)
SONG LYRICS BY PAUL SIMON • ILLUSTRATIONS BY KEITH HENRY BROWN
Paul Simon's anthem to New York City is the joyful basis for this live-for-the-day children's picture book, providing a perfect vehicle to teach kids to appreciate life's little gifts.

African
SONG LYRICS BY PETER TOSH • ILLUSTRATIONS BY RACHEL MOSS
A beautiful children's picture book featuring the lyrics of Peter Tosh's global classic celebrating people of African descent.

(Sittin' on) The Dock of the Bay
SONG LYRICS BY OTIS REDDING AND STEVE CROPPER • IILLUSTRATIONS BY KAITLYN SHEA O'CONNOR
Otis Redding and Steve Cropper's timeless ode to never-ending days is given fresh new life in this heartwarming picture book.

Don't Stop
SONG LYRICS BY CHRISTINE McVIE • ILLUSTRATIONS BY NUSHA ASHJAEE
McVie's classic song about keeping one's chin up and rolling with life's punches is beautifully adapted to an uplifting children's book.

Dream Weaver
SONG LYRICS BY GARY WRIGHT • ILLUSTRATIONS BY ROB SAYEGH JR.
Gary Wright's hit song is reimagined as a fantastical picture book to delight dreamers of all ages.

Good Vibrations
SONG LYRICS BY MIKE LOVE AND BRIAN WILSON • ILLUSTRATIONS BY PAUL HOPPE
Mike Love and Brian Wilson's world-famous song, gloriously illustrated by Paul Hoppe, will bring smiles to the faces of children and parents alike.

I Will Survive
SONG LYRICS BY DINO FEKARIS AND FREDERICK J. PERREN • ILLUSTRATIONS BY KAITLYN SHEA O'CONNOR
disco hit sensation "I Will Survive"—popularized by Gloria Gaynor—comes ing picture book featuring an alien princess living life on her own terms.